DANNY'S BIRTHDAY

Edith Kunhardt

A TRUMPET CLUB SPECIAL EDITION

Published by The Trumpet Club
a division of Bantam Doubleday Dell Publishing Group, Inc.
666 Fifth Avenue, New York, New York 10103

ISBN: 0-440-84193-3

Reprinted by arrangement with Greenwillow Books,
a division of William Morrow & Company, Inc.
Printed in the United States of America
February 1990

10 9 8 7 6 5 4 3 2 1
UPC

The four-color preseparated art was printed in
yellow, red, black and blue.
The typeface is Avant Garde Gothic Book.

For Mark Pagels

It is Danny's birthday.
He is five years old.

Danny's father is making a tape
of Danny's party. He shoots Danny
in his new birthday clothes.

Danny's friends come to his party.

His friends are Lucy, Mark, and Joshua.
They put the presents in a pile.

Danny and his friends
play a game.
It is called Spider Web.
Danny follows the green wool.

At the end of the wool is a present.

It is time to eat. Everyone sits at the table.
There are party hats and blowers.
When the cake comes, Danny blows out
one, two, three, four, five candles,
and one to grow on.

Now it is time to open the presents.

Danny gets a kite from Lucy.
"I love it!" he shouts.

Danny opens a flashlight that flashes
green and red. It is from Mark.
"Oh good!" he cries.

Danny gets a watch that turns
into a robot from Joshua.
"Just what I wanted!" says Danny.

Now Lucy, Mark, and Joshua get
their goody bags. The party is over.

"Goodbye!" they call.
"Happy birthday, Danny!"

Danny's father has taped the whole party.

Now he plays the tape on the TV.

There is Danny in his new birthday clothes.

There are Lucy, Mark, and Joshua.

There are the Spider Web, the cake,
the presents, and saying goodbye.
Danny wants to see it again.
He watches two more times.

Early the next morning, Danny gets up.

He goes to the TV in his mother and father's room.

He turns it on. He watches the party.

The third time Danny watches, Mother and Father make him turn off the set.

That afternoon, Danny
watches the party again.
He watches it over and over.

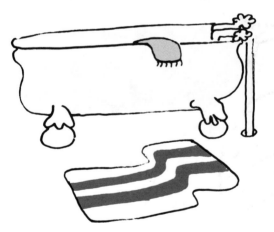

After his bath, Danny wants to watch
the party again. But the tape is way
up high. He can't reach it.

"I want to see my party," says Danny.

"Later," says his mother.

"*Much* later," says his father. "Let's just try and remember it," he adds.

"Okay," says Danny after a minute.
"I remembered it.
Now can I see the tape?"
So they all sit down and watch the
tape one more time.